Allen B

& the Open Gate

Written By **Matthew Crosby**

Illustrated By **Nick Francis DiFonzo**

1

If you've ever been on a train heading across the countryside, and you're the sort who tends to look out the window instead of straight ahead into the seat of the fellow in front of you (and I'm not a betting man, but if I were a betting man I'd be willing to bet as much as about seventeen dollars that you are), then you're sure to have seen, once or twice, the sight of a hillside spotted with little white clouds which aren't clouds at all, but sheep.

This story takes place on one of those hillsides and it's about one of the sheep who lives there and his name is Allen B. But before I tell you about him,

YOU'LL NEED TO KNOW ONE OR TWO THINGS ABOUT SHEEP...

Sheep are very agreeable -- as a matter of fact, they tend to agree with just about anything that anybody ever says or does. You'd be hard-pressed to find anyone at all with an unkind word for them as people in general.

But like everyone else, sheep aren't perfect, and if they've got one problem that's more of a hassle than any other, it's this one: It is next to impossible for a sheep to keep a single thought in his head for more than about one second or so.

You might call them dim-witted if it weren't such a nasty thing to say, but you'd be wrong. They're not. They just have very, very, very short memories.

2

This is why Allen B had been staring at the pasture gate for so long. Because he kept forgetting why he was staring at it. He forgot and remembered and forgot, again and again for who knows how long -- hours maybe, until he had the curious and unfamiliar sensation of a single thought sticking in his brain for more than one second and the thought was this:

The gate was open.

The pasture gate was never open. At least not in as long as Allen B could remember, which of course was not very long. It seemed to him that something ought to be done, and that that thing might just as well be to walk through it because, after all, (he still remembered!) it was open. And just wide enough, he thought, for a sheep to pass through. And why not? Allen B had been everywhere in the pasture.

He'd been down by the gully where the stream
ran past.

He'd been at the foot of the hill where daisies grew when the weather was nice.

He'd been under the big elm tree where Snag, the old plow horse stood all day looking out above the ancient stone wall at whatever you could see if you were tall enough, which Allen B had wondered about, but never remembered to ask him.

He'd been everywhere in the pasture. Why shouldn't he be outside of it too?

On the other hand, nobody else seemed to be walking through the gate. This meant a great deal to Allen B because sheep, as a rule, only like to do things that other sheep are doing. It's a handy way of making sure that no one ever upsets anybody else or gets out of line. It also makes you wonder how any of them ever do anything in the first place. Anyway, it would make me wonder if I were you.

So Allen B, taking great care to keep what was on his mind on his mind, set out to find someone who thought walking through the gate sounded like as good an idea as it did to him, which was very very good, and getting better the more he thought about it.

3

He found his brother Charles B grazing in the southeastern corner of the pasture. Charles B could always be found there. It was the only part of the pasture where the sun shone all day long, and Charles B stayed there specifically to avoid ever having to move around.

Allen B was sure that Charles B would want to walk through the gate with him, if only for the change of scenery. It must be so boring to stay in the same place all the time, after all. Don't you think so?

When Allen B found him, Charles B had just finished eating. He was always either eating or finishing eating or getting ready to eat. A long strand of grass was stuck to the scruff of his chin.

"Hello Charles B," Allen B said cheerfully.
"Hello Allen B," said Charles B.
"Beautiful day," said Allen B, and it really was. Charles B agreed that it was beautiful.

"Charles B, I have a question for you."
"All right" said Charles B.
"Well, I was wondering..."
"Yes?" said Charles B.
"...Wondering if you thought you might..."
"Yes?" said Charles B.
"Oh no," said Allen B.
"Oh no what?" said Charles B.

It was gone! His thought was gone! He'd lost it just like that!

"I, I can't...remember," said Allen B, feeling terribly disappointed in himself. If you've ever forgotten something you were trying hard to remember, you'll know just how he felt.

"Well it must not have been very important, anyway," said Charles B.

"It was!" Allen B cried.

"It was very important!"

For a good while they stood there, staring straight ahead as sheep tend to do when there isn't something else going on. Allen B was trying desperately to remember what he had forgotten. Charles B wasn't thinking about anything in particular.

A light breeze blew down off the hill above the pasture and Allen B noticed the piece of grass on Charles B's chin blowing softly sideways and then swinging back into place. It happened again and then a third time. Back and forth. Out and in. It reminded him of something ... 'What was it?' he wondered. Something that opened and closed. Opened and closed.

Just

like

a

GATE!

He remembered! The gate was open!

"The gate is open!" he exclaimed, leaping into the air as he did.

"What gate?" asked Charles B, sounding a little bored, and right away, Allen B wondered if he'd been the right person to ask after all.

"The pasture gate!" said Allen B. "It's open! I thought the two of us might walk through it and have a look outside. What do you say?"

"Well," said Charles B, "I don't recall having seen any pasture gate, but if there were one, I don't know what business a sheep would have walking through it."

Allen B couldn't help feeling a little bit disappointed. Even more than a little bit.

Charles B went back to eating and Allen B knew already that it was no use trying to convince him. "Oh well," he said. "Never mind then."

"Never mind about what?" asked Charles B with his mouth full of grass as Allen B started off.

4

Making his way swiftly across the pasture, Allen B repeating to himself as he trotted along, "The gate is open, the gate is open," so as not to forget again.

When he found his Very Best Friend Abilene, she was rolling around in a pile of hay at the foot of the big hill and laughing at a funny thought she had already forgotten. Apart from their adventures all over the pasture, rolling around in the hay was her favorite thing to do, and Allen B's too, and they did it together all the time.

The two of them were very much alike in more ways than they could count, and being sheep, it would of course have been very difficult for them to try. They even looked like one another. In fact, Allen B and Abilene were so much alike that sometimes even they themselves forgot who was who. It didn't help one bit that their names sounded so similar, believe me.

In as long as Allen B could remember, which was not very long, they'd never disagreed about anything, so he was sure that Abilene would want to walk through the gate with him. All he'd have to do was ask. And remember!

"Good morning, Allen B!" Abilene exclaimed when he walked up, forgetting for a moment that they'd seen each other already that day.

"The gate is open, the gate is open," said Allen B to himself.

"What?" said Abilene.

"Sorry," said Allen B. "Hello, Allen B -- I mean, Hello Abilene. The gate is open."

"The pasture gate?" asked Abilene.

"Yes!" said Allen B. He thought it was a heck of a good start that she knew which gate he meant. "I thought you and I might walk through and have a look at what's outside. It'll be a new adventure!"

Abilene turned to gaze across the pasture in the direction of the gate with a worried look.

"Is something wrong?" Allen B asked.

"Oh Allen B," said Abilene. "Couldn't we have an adventure inside the pasture? It's such a good day for one, and, well, what if isn't such a good day out...there?"

Allen B couldn't deny either that he knew nothing about the world outside of the pasture gate or that it certainly was a fine day inside it, but it seemed to him that these weren't reasons to stay so much as reasons not to go, if you know what I mean.

"I don't know, Abilene," said Allen B. "That's what I wanted to find out, I guess. I thought you might too."

But he could see that she didn't. He could also see that she seemed to feel a little badly about it, and he certainly didn't want that, after all. But it worried him that she didn't want to go. Just as Abilene had always agreed with him, he had always agreed with her right back. If she didn't think it was a good idea, maybe it wasn't.

"It's alright," he said before she could reply. "Maybe tomorrow."

"I'm sorry, Abilene" said Abilene, meaning to say 'Allen B'. But he was already on his way across the pasture again, and focused hard on the thought of the open gate, which was becoming more and more stuck in his brain with every passing minute.

5

He found Snag standing, as usual, under the big elm tree swatting flies with his tail and looking out above the stone wall. Swatting flies was the main thing Snag did. He was very old. Nobody remembered anybody who remembered a time before Snag came to the pasture. He seemed to Allen B to be as old as the wall itself. He was also the one and only horse Allen B had ever known. When he remembered to, he sometimes wondered whether all horses were as old as Snag. They aren't of course, but you couldn't blame him, could you? If you didn't know as many horses as you do, which I bet is about six, you might wonder the same thing.

Snag gave a little snort to say hello and then, for a while, the two of them stood there without speaking. As a rule, not speaking comes much more naturally to sheep than to human people, and they do it pretty regularly, but Allen B especially enjoyed not speaking with Snag. He didn't speak with Snag as often as he could, in fact. They would stand -- Snag gazing out over the old wall and Allen B gazing right into it -- for hours at a time, in total silence.

But today, Allen B had a question or two for Snag. Snag being so old and having so little to say had given Allen B the impression that he was very wise, which if you ask me, wasn't a bad impression to have.

"Snag?" said Allen B.

"Yes, Allen B?" said old Snag.

"What's out there?"

"Out where?" said Snag.

"Over the wall," said Allen B. "Outside the pasture."

Snag slowly tilted his massive head to get an eye on Allen B, who was himself looking more or less straight up in order to see Snag's face. He was very anxious to hear the answer.

Snag seemed to be thinking very hard about the question, which certainly seemed simple enough to Allen B. The old horse looked back out over the wall, and after a few moments, answered for some reason as if he were talking to himself. "Another pasture," he said quietly.

You might be thinking that Allen B found this answer disappointing or at least a little dull, but you must remember that he loved pastures, as far as he knew, about as much as anything in the world. The idea of another one -- right outside the gate, at that -- was terrifically and terribly exciting. His mind was already racing. He wondered what animals might live there and if they ate grass and whether they loved going on adventures as much as he did and whether one of them might himself come walking through that gate any minute. He was so excited he almost leapt into the air.

And yet there was something about Snag's answer -- not what he said, but in his voice when he said it -- that bothered Allen B. He didn't know a word for it because it wasn't something that sheep have any use for, but you and I would call it sadness. So instead of asking about the new pasture, which he wanted very badly to do, Allen B, trying not to sound too excited, said, "Is that all? Is there anything else?" Straight away, he realized that it was itself a fine question and felt very proud to have asked it.

"Yes," said Snag quietly. "There are other things. There are rivers and men and plows and roads and work and fences and many more things too."

"Can you tell me about them?" said Allen B, really wanting to say 'all of them', but trying to sound as serious as Snag.

"I can't," said Snag.

Allen B was surprised and a little bit disappointed by this. Even more than a little bit. "Why not?"

"Because I'm afraid anything I had to tell you wouldn't mean a thing unless you'd seen them for yourself," Snag said, and then snorted.

"Oh," said Allen B, and just as he was about to walk away to do some thinking about this, Snag spoke again.

"Allen B," he said.

"Yes, Snag?" said Allen B.

"Are you thinking of going out to see them for yourself?"

In as long as Allen B could remember, which of course was not very long, Snag had never once asked him a question. It was always the other way around.

"Well I don't know," said Allen B, wondering suddenly if horses could see inside other people's brains. "That's what I was trying to decide. It's just that no one else seems to think it's a good idea. Why is that?"

"Because you," said Snag, "are not everyone else. And everyone else isn't you."

You might think it was a sort of an obvious thing to say, but Allen B had never exactly looked at things quite that way. Sheep aren't inclined to think those kinds of thoughts.

Then Snag, in a not unfriendly way, snorted the snort that he snorted when he was ready to not talk again. Allen B, having a great deal to think about, left him there and went over to have another look at the gate.

5

Along the way, the terrible thought appeared in his mind that someone might have closed it. Terrified, he began to run and ran as fast as sheep legs will carry a person.

When he reached the gate, it was still standing open, just as before. He breathed a sigh of great relief and settled down into the grass to think with his eyes locked on the gate, promising himself he wouldn't look away again until he had decided what he was going to do about it. For the first time, it occurred to Allen B that having so many thoughts in his head meant having some bad ones as well as the good ones.

Without realizing it, Allen B had become extremely fond of Having His Own Ideas About Things, and now he was having some good ones. About Abilene and Charles B, about his pasture and the new one out there, about himself.

If he was going to walk out the gate, it meant doing something really and truly on his own for the very first time. If you've ever done something really and truly on your own, then you'll know just how he felt. There would surely be new things to see, but some of them might be as unpleasant as a closed gate. Staying, on the other hand, would be so easy. He and Abilene might even have time for an adventure before lunch. If he was lucky, he'd have forgotten by bedtime that the gate was ever open at all.

But just then, the sun came out from behind a cloud and Allen B felt it on his back and remembered that some things don't go away even when you walk through gates, and that he himself was one of those things.

And in a moment he knew that, for a little while at least, there was no more thinking to be done because he'd made his decision.

And I'm not a betting man, but I'll bet you know what it was.

Published in the United States
by Xist Publishing
www.xistpublishing.com

xist Publishing

Made in the USA
Middletown, DE
12 December 2017